Where's My House?
- Sierra National Forest -

A story inspired by the
compassion and resiliency of children.

Created by Junior Authors from around the world, and Susie Harder, M.A., CCC-SLP
Illustrated by Lily Liu

Welcome to Junior Authors

ABOUT THE FOUNDER
Susie Harder, M.A., CCC-SLP

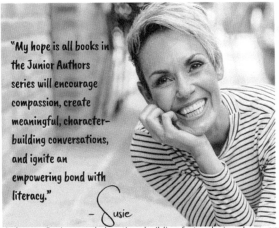

"My hope is all books in the Junior Authors series will encourage compassion, create meaningful, character-building conversations, and ignite an empowering bond with literacy."

— Susie

At home, Susie spends her time building forts, playing chase, and doing silly dance moves with her two kids and fun-loving husband. She loves nachos, scavenger hunts, and cozy snuggles at bedtime. Her dog's name is Wrigley (after the Chicago Cubs Wrigley Field) and is like a real-life Charlie! When Susie goes to work, she is a Speech-Language Pathologist who loves helping children who stutter. She teaches kids how to be confident and brave, even if they're feeling shy or unsure. Susie has an endless supply of smiles, wants every child to feel heard and gives great high-fives. Rumor has it that she has an entire room of games at her office and claims to be the Connect 4 Champion!

This book is gratefully and lovingly dedicated to:
My husband, Bryan- Thank you for being incredibly supportive and always making me laugh!
My children, Hudson and Allie- May you always use your talents to help others and know the true value of family and home.

— Susie

Xav, my husband and Frincine, my dear mom- Thank you for making me feel loved and encouraged all the time.
Loona, My sweet daughter and my sunshine- Your happiness inspires me everyday.

— Lily

CALLING ALL TEACHERS!

Official
JUNIOR AUTHOR
is awarded to

Join our global community of schools!

Invite your students to help create our next book as Official Junior Authors!

HOW IT WORKS

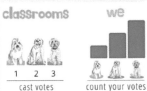

classrooms
1 2 3
cast votes

we
count your votes

illustrator
uses winning votes

together
we publish a book!

DID YOU KNOW?

Every aspect of this book was lovingly crafted with the input from children around the globe. What began an educationally based, social-emotional support for local children who lost homes in the 2020 California Creek Fire, has quickly grown into a global literacy-building project. See how many pieces of children's artwork you can spot!

**NOMINATE YOUR SCHOOL &
DOWNLOAD FREE PRINTABLE ACTIVITIES :**
WWW.WHERESMYHOUSE.ORG

This book was created by

JUNIOr AUTHOr

_____ _____
Name   Age

This Junior Author is known for being:

CREATE AND DESIGN YOUR LIST! HERE ARE A FEW IDEAS FROM AVA:
Compassionate, resilient, open-minded, patient, kind, caring,
grateful, supportive, respectful, courageous, calm, positive, helpful, creative.

LOOK!
This book is signed by a
JUNIOr AUTHOR!

A special dedication to all children who lost homes to the Creek Fire.

As the next generation of community leaders, these children are being celebrated for their joyful contributions toward strengthening, unifying, and rebuilding the community and its forest.

For a complete list of Featured Junior Authors, please visit WheresMyHouse.org

Ava and Charlie loved spending time together.

Surprising Charlie was a neighborhood tradition. Everyone knew exactly what to do when they heard Ava announce... "DOG PILE!"

But today, their whole world was about to change.

They were out exploring when they heard sirens and ran home.

"What happened?" wondered Ava.
"It looks like a fire burnt our land. And Charlie... oh, no!
Your house is gone, too."

"I'm so sorry, Charlie," she whispered.
"Everything looks and feels so different now."

The next morning, they walked through the neighborhood.
Ava noticed the sadness in Charlie's face.
"You miss your house, don't you? I bet you miss your toys
and your bed, too."

What could Ava do to help?
She wished she could make his house magically reappear.

"Squirrel, please hold my hat. Let's get to work before Charlie wakes up!"

Ava and the animals worked tirelessly.

"Charlie, we made something for you."
Charlie's eyes widened with excitement.

"This house will feel different because it is new.
It's special, though, because we made it for you.

Do you see any of your favorite things?"

Ava was ready to celebrate with a suprise dog pile!
Just then, something caught her eye.

They built a house for Cat with all her favorite things.

Ava was more excited than ever for their surprise dog pile.
"Bird, please tell the animals we're ready! "
Just then, something caught her eye.

Two friends still need help..
Do you see who?
Take a look around.
What can Ava do?

They built houses for Squirrel and Bird with all their favorite things.

Finally, time for their celebratory
dog pile. Just then...
something caught Ava's eye.

Ava's yard was feeling more like home, but her heart sank as she peered over the fence.

"When bad things happen
And our friends feel blue,
We have to decide
What WE'RE going to do."

With everyone together, the gray seemed to fade away. Although the old houses were gone, the most important people were even closer than before.

"Welcome home friends."

Before Ava could finish, something caught her eye.
All the animals surprised Ava with...

The happiest, cuddliest, and most slobbery dog pile they'd ever had!

Made in the USA
Las Vegas, NV
25 September 2024

95778949R00021